MONSTER HEROES

BOY UNDER THE BED

BY BLAKE HOENA
ILLUSTRATED BY DAVE BARDIN

STONE ARCH BOOKS
a capstone imprint

Monster Heroes is published by
Stone Arch Books, a Capstone Imprint
1710 Roe Crest Drive
North Mankato, Minnesota 56003
www.mycapstone.com

Library of Congress Cataloging-in-Publication data
is available on the Library of Congress website.
ISBN: 978-1-4965-6414-6 (library binding)
ISBN: 978-1-4965-6418-4 (paperback)
ISBN: 978-1-4965-6422-1 (eBook PDF)

Summary: Will the ghost is beyond scared when he hears noises
in his room after he goes to bed. A thump from under the bed and a
thud from the closet lead Will to discover a human boy and girl in his
bedroom! He needs to get them out before his scary sister finds them.
Will calls his friends and the Monster Heroes come to the rescue!

Book design by: Ted Williams
Photo credit: Shutterstock: Kasha_malasha,
design element, popular business, design element

TABLE OF CONTENTS

MINA (the Vampire)

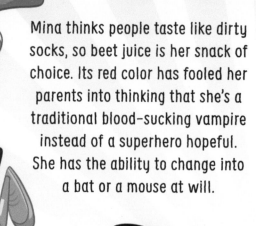

Mina thinks people taste like dirty socks, so beet juice is her snack of choice. Its red color has fooled her parents into thinking that she's a traditional blood-sucking vampire instead of a superhero hopeful. She has the ability to change into a bat or a mouse at will.

Brian is the brainy one amongst his friends. Unlike other zombies, Brian prefers tofu to brains. No matter what sort of trouble is brewing, Brian always comes up with a plan to save the day, like a true superhero.

BRIAN (the Zombie)

WILL (the Ghost)

Will is quite shy. Luckily he can turn invisible any time he wants because he is a ghost. When Will is doing good deeds, he likes to remain unseen. His invisibility helps him act brave like a real superhero.

With a wave of her wand and a poetic chant, Linda can reverse any magical curse. She hopes to use her magic to help people, just like a superhero would.

LINDA (the Witch)

CHAPTER 1

A SCARY DARE

"Yaaawwwnnn," Will moaned.

"Time for bed."

He curled up in his blankets.

Just as his eyes were about to close,

something bumped and thumped

under his bed.

Bu-bump THUMP!

Bu-bump THUMP!

"W-w-what was that?" Will whispered.

He sat up and looked around, but he did not see anything strange or unusual.

"Must be my imagination," he said.

Will often imagined frightening things. Once, he dreamed that giant moths were trying to eat his sheet. Scary! Another time, he thought a wiggling blob of mayonnaise was about to fall on him.

"Yaaawwwnnn," Will moaned again. He lay back down in bed.

Just as he closed his eyes, something rustled in his closet.

Rustle-rustle THUD!

Rustle-rustle THUD!

"Who-who-who's there?" Will said as he sat up again.

There was no reply.

Will was no longer tired. Now he was afraid. Scary noises were coming from under his bed. Frightening sounds were coming from his closet.

He did not know what to do.

Just then his bed began to bounce up and down.

Bumpity bump bump THUMP!

Will pulled his blankets tightly around him. He shook in fear. A moment later, he saw a hand, eyes, and a nose.

A boy! A real human boy was hiding under Will's bed.

"Are you a ghost?" the boy asked.

"Y-y-yes," Will replied.

"That's so cool!" a shout came from his closet.

A girl! A real human girl was hiding in Will's closet!

"What are you doing here?" Will asked them.

"Our friends said this house was haunted," the girl said.

"They dared us to sneak inside," the boy said.

A SCARIER SISTER

"You are lucky you didn't hide in my sister's room," Will said.

"Is she a ghost too?" the girl asked.

"We wouldn't be afraid," the boy said.

Will shuddered. "Yes, you would," he said. "She's not nice like me."

Will was a ghost who did not like to scare people. His friends actually tried to help people. They wanted to be like superheroes, not scary monsters.

"My sister, Dolly, would scare you to death!" Will exclaimed.

Just then, there was a knock at the door.

"Will, are you awake?" came an eerie voice.

"It's my sister. Hide," Will whispered.

The boy squirmed back under the bed. The girl leaped back into the closet.

Will picked up his phone. He texted one word to his friends: *Help!* Then he crawled back under his blankets.

"Come in, Dolly," he said.

In walked a life-sized doll. It was his sister, Dolly. As she stood in the doorway, her head spun all the way around.

"I can't fall asleep," Dolly
said. "Can you please tell me
a bedtime story?"

"Sure," Will said. "What kind of story would you like me to tell you?"

Dolly's head spun around as she thought about it.

"A story about scaring people," she said with a grin.

"Okay," Will said. "Once there was a boy hiding under a bed, and a girl hiding in a closet."

THE SCARIEST STORY

"What happens next?" Dolly asked. "Do they get eaten?"

"No, no, no," Will said.

Just then, a bat fluttered through Will's window. It was Will's friend Mina, the vampire.

"A bat flew into the room," Will continued. "It flew all over the place!"

As Will told his story, Mina swooped and whirled. She flew around and around the room. Dolly's head spun as she watched the bat.

"Psst," Linda called to Will from the window. Linda was a good witch. She held up her wand and waved it in the air.

"What happens next?" Dolly asked.

"There was a witch," Will said, "who cast a spell."

"Abarah kah-zeer, abarah kah-zoor," Linda quietly chanted. "Your head will spin off and fall to the floor."

Dolly continued to watch the bat fly around. Her head continued to spin around, until it came loose and fell to the floor.

PLOP!

"Hey!" Dolly shouted.

As her head rolled out the door, her body chased after it.

"The plan is working!" a whisper came from the window. "She's been distracted."

Will turned to see his friend Brian, the zombie.

"Out the window. Go!" Brian said to the boy and girl.

Brian and Linda helped them crawl through the window. Then the boy and girl ran off into the night. For some reason they weren't even scared.

"Humans are strange," Brian said.

Will leaned out the window to thank his friends.

"You saved the day!" Will said.

"Just like real superheroes," Linda said.

"Now what?" Mina asked.

"Yaaawwwwnnn," Will moaned. "Back to bed, I guess."

DAVE BARDIN

Dave Bardin studied illustration at Cal State Fullerton while working as an art teacher. As an artist, Dave has worked on many different projects for television, books, comics, and animation. In his spare time Dave enjoys watching documentaries, listening to podcasts, traveling, and spending time with friends and family. He works out of Los Angeles, California.

BLAKE HOENA

Blake Hoena grew up in central Wisconsin, where he wrote stories about robots conquering the moon and trolls lumbering around the woods behind his parents' house. He now lives in Minnesota and continues to write about fun things like space aliens and superheroes. Blake has written more than fifty chapter books and graphic novels for children.

GLOSSARY

chant—to say a phrase over and over

distract—to draw attention away from

flutter—to flap wings quickly

haunted—to have ghosts, such as a haunted house

imagination—to form a picture in your mind

rustle—to make a soft sound

shudder—to shake

spell—a type of magic

squirm—to make lots of movement

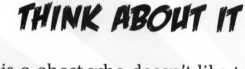

THINK ABOUT IT

1. Will is a ghost who doesn't like to scare people. If you were a ghost, how would you spend your time?

2. Dolly asks Will to tell her a bedtime story. Turn to a partner and tell your own version of Will's bedtime story.

3. What is something you were scared of when you were younger but that you are not afraid of anymore? How did you overcome your fear?

WRITE ABOUT IT

1. Dolly sounds super scary! Write the beginning to a spooky story that features her as the main character.

2. What do you think a ghost's bedtime routine is like? Make a list of things you do before getting into bed. Now make a list for Will. What might be the same? What is different?

3. Pretend that you are one of the kids from Will's room. Write a thank-you letter to Will for helping you escape.

THE FUN DOESN'T STOP HERE!

Discover more at
www.capstonekids.com